Noddy is Far Too Busy

Collins

An Imprint of HarperCollins*Publishers*

MARTH

TESSIE BEAR

MR PLOD

MASTER TUBBY BEAR

ONKEY

SLY

MR WOBBLY MAN

BUMPY DOG

It was a lively afternoon in Toyland . . .

Noddy was driving Mr and Mrs Noah to the station. They were going to visit Mr Noah's sister and, since they were staying the night, Noddy had promised to look after all their animals for them.

"You will feed them now, won't you, Noddy?" Mrs Noah asked anxiously as Noddy parked outside the station.

"I promise I'll go to your Ark this evening," said Noddy.

After dropping off Mr and Mrs Noah at the station, Noddy drove to Market Square in search of more passengers.

He arrived there just as Tessie Bear was trying on a scarf at Dinah Doll's stall.

"Oh it's a beautiful scarf, Dinah!" exclaimed Tessie Bear admiringly.

Noddy thought the scarf looked beautiful on Tessie Bear as well, and urged her to buy it, but she told him that she did not have enough money. The scarf cost twelve sixpences!

"I shall have to save up for it," she remarked sadly as she handed it back to Dinah Doll.

"Oh Dinah, I should love to give Tessie that scarf," Noddy sighed as soon as she had left, "but I don't have enough sixpences either!"

"Well, I'll pay you two sixpences if you take this parcel to the train station," said Dinah Doll.

"I'll go right away!" Noddy replied excitedly.

While Noddy was at the station, he saw the strangest sight – a walking plant!

The plant talked as well, and it told Noddy that he was the very person it was looking for!

"Ah, Noddy!" exclaimed the plant. "The very toy!"

"Oh!" cried Noddy, quite startled. "A talking plant!"

But the plant explained that it was not a talking plant at all!

"It is I, Miss Pink Cat!" said a voice from behind all the leaves. "I wish to give you two sixpences. You must take me to the garage!"

Mr Sparks was quite delighted by Miss Pink Cat's plant and suggested that the two of them should go and find a suitable place for it.

"Noddy, will you clean my car and look after the garage while Miss Pink Cat and I choose the best place for her wonderful plant?" asked Mr Sparks.

Of course, Noddy was only too happy to accept Mr Sparks' offer. It meant he would have some more sixpences towards the cost of Tessie Bear's scarf!

"My! You have been working hard, Noddy!" Mr Sparks exclaimed when he came back to find his car gleaming like new. "I think I'll give you an extra sixpence!"

By now, Noddy was looking so tired that Mr Sparks told him to go straight home to bed.

"Oh I will, but I'm sure I have another job..." Noddy tried to think what this other job might be. He was sure it was very important!

"I wish I could remember..." he mumbled as he trudged wearily towards his bed.

The next morning, while Noddy was having a bit of a lie in, the Toy Town folk were waking up to discover all sorts of strange things.

"Something chewed my hedge during the night," Jumbo complained to Mr Plod. "There's a big hole in it!"

Mr Sparks complained that something had chewed his new plant as well, and Dinah Doll reported that she had woken up to find Market Square covered with muddy footprints!

"Strange goings-on indeed!" Mr Plod remarked solemnly, not sure what to make of it all.

Armed with his magnifying glass, Mr Plod immediately went looking for clues.

"Have you lost something, Mr Plod?" Noddy asked on seeing him.

"No, Noddy," he replied gravely, "I'm investigating muddy footprints and strange goings-on!"

Mr Plod was just telling Noddy that there was a reward for anyone who solved the mystery of the chewed hedge and the muddy footprints, when they heard a piercing scream.

"Help! Help!" cried a voice in distress.

Noddy and Mr Plod both raced off in the direction of the cries, which led them to Miss Pink Cat's house.

"Help! Help!" Miss Pink Cat shrieked again. "Mr Noah's lion – he will not let me pass!"

"Mr Lion, kindly let Miss Pink Cat pass," ordered Mr Plod.

"No, I won't. Lions like guarding, and shut away in the Ark I've never had the chance," the lion replied.

Mr Plod wondered how the lion had escaped from the Ark. Only then did Noddy realise what it was that he had forgotten to do the previous evening.

"Oh no!" he gasped, horror-struck. "I was meant to look after the Ark for Mr and Mrs Noah!"

The lion was not the only animal who had escaped from Mr Noah's Ark. So had the zebra!

"Please! Move out of the way!" Milko said to the zebra as he tried to pass. "I've got the morning milk to deliver!"

When Noddy arrived, he became more desperate than ever.

"There's not meant to be a real zebra crossing here!" he pleaded with the stubborn animal. "You must let me take you back to the Ark!"

But the zebra did not want to go back – he rather liked the way his black and white stripes matched those painted on the road!

There were even more problems at the café, where Mr Noah's giraffes were sitting together at one of the tables, blocking the way for everyone.

"Now, what shall we have for lunch?" one giraffe asked the other as they looked at the menu.

Realising that it was these two giraffes who had chewed Jumbo's hedge and Mr Sparks' plant, Noddy decided that he had better own up to Mr Plod.

"I'm afraid the strange goings-on are my fault!" he declared. "I was meant to look after the animals for Mr and Mrs Noah, but I was so busy I forgot, and now they've escaped!"

Noddy and Mr Plod set off to try to persuade all the animals to go back to the Ark. They started with the lion lying on Miss Pink Cat's doorstep.

But the lion took no notice of them – he was quite comfortable where he was!

Noddy and Mr Plod were just about to give up when Tessie Bear arrived, carrying a cake she had baked for Noddy.

"Do I smell fruit and nut cake?" the lion asked with a lick of his lips.

"I baked it for Noddy's tea," Tessie Bear replied. "You can have a slice if you let Noddy take you to the Ark."

Taking another sniff of the delicious cake, the lion decided this was a very good deal. "Oh let's hurry!" he exclaimed with an eager grin. "I can't wait."

Tessie Bear offered a slice of her cake to the zebra as well, and he too agreed to let Noddy lead him home.

It was exactly the same with the giraffes at the café. Not one of Mr and Mrs Noah's animals could resist the delicious smell of Tessie Bear's cake!

So, when Noddy and Tessie Bear went to collect Mr and Mrs Noah from the station, they were able to report that all their animals were fit and well.

"We've just fed them, Mrs Noah," Tessie told her quite truthfully, "and they've all really enjoyed themselves." She decided not to mention that the animals had spent the night away from the Ark!

Before hurrying back to the Ark, Mr and Mrs Noah gave Noddy some sixpences for looking after their animals.

"Thank you, Mr Noah!" said Noddy with a delighted smile.

Noddy was especially delighted because the sixpences from Mr and Mrs Noah meant that he now had exactly twelve sixpences in all.

"So I'll be able to buy that scarf for you!" he told Tessie Bear excitedly, hurrying her along to Dinah Doll's stall.

"I'm sorry there wasn't any of my cake left for you," Tessie Bear told Noddy later that day.

"Never mind!" Noddy chuckled. "If we hadn't fed the cake to Mr Noah's animals, I wouldn't have earned those extra sixpences. And then you wouldn't have had this lovely warm scarf!"

This edition first published in Great Britain by HarperCollins Publishers Ltd in 2000

1 3 5 7 9 10 8 6 4 2

ISBN: 0 00 136181 3

A CIP catalogue for this title is available from the British Library.

The HarperCollins website address is:
www.**fire**and**water**.com

Reproduction by Graphic Studio S.r.l. Verona
Printed in Italy by Garzanti Verga S.r.l.

MORE NODDY BOOKS FOR YOU TO ENJOY

Noddy and the Artists

Noddy and the Bouncing Ball

Noddy is Caught in a Storm

Noddy and the Driving Lesson

Noddy and the Goblins

Noddy and the Magic Watch

Noddy and the Noisy Drum

Noddy the Nurse

Noddy and the Singing Bush

Noddy Tells a Story

Noddy Tidies Toyland

Noddy and the Treasure Map